This Walker book belongs to:

_____

_____

_____

For Robyn – J.E.
For Hugo – V.C.

First published 2005 by Walker Books Ltd
87 Vauxhall Walk, London SE11 5HJ

This edition published 2017

2 4 6 8 10 9 7 5 3 1

Text © 2005 Jonathan Emmett
Illustrations © 2005 Vanessa Cabban

The right of Jonathan Emmett and Vanessa Cabban to be
identified as author and illustrator respectively of this work
has been asserted by them in accordance with
the Copyright, Designs and Patents Act 1988

This book has been typeset in Beta Bold

Printed in China

British Library Cataloguing in Publication Data:
a catalogue record for this book is available from the British Library

ISBN 978-1-4063-7311-0

You can find out more about Jonathan Emmett's books
by visiting his website at www.scribblestreet.co.uk

www.walker.co.uk

No Place Like Home

Jonathan Emmett

illustrated by Vanessa Cabban

WALKER BOOKS
AND SUBSIDIARIES
LONDON • BOSTON • SYDNEY • AUCKLAND

"Hot-diggerty!"

said Mole, as he climbed

out of the ground one morning.

It was a beautiful day.

The sun was shining.

And there were flowers everywhere.

Suddenly Mole's burrow seemed

very small and dark and dull.

"Why should I live underground,"

Mole said to himself,

"when I could live

somewhere BIG

and BRIGHT

and BEAUTIFUL instead!"

And Mole
set off in search
of a new home.

He hadn't
gone far when
he came across
Hedgehog.

"Hello, Mole,"
said Hedgehog. "Where are you off to?"

"I'm looking for a new home," explained Mole.
"Somewhere
BIG and
BRIGHT and
BEAUTIFUL."

"I know just the place!"
said Hedgehog.
"Follow me!"

"So what do you think?"
asked Hedgehog,
as they crawled into a hollow log.
Mole tried to feel at home
in the log, but the wind
was whistling right
through it.

"Well,"
said Mole, shivering,
"it is very BIG – but it's too draughty
for me. I'd like somewhere
a little more snug."

"What's up?"
asked Squirrel.

"I'm looking
for a new home,"
explained Mole.
"Somewhere
BRIGHT
and BEAUTIFUL."

"And SNUG,"
added
Hedgehog.

Mole and Hedgehog
had just crawled
out of the log
when they saw
Squirrel.

"I know just the place!"
said Squirrel.
"Follow me!"

"So what do you think?"
said Squirrel, as Mole clambered
into an empty bird's nest.

Mole tried to feel
at home in the nest. But he was
too afraid of falling out.

"Well," he said, "it is very BRIGHT –
but it's too dangerous for me.
I'd like somewhere a little
more safe."

Hedgehog, Squirrel and Mole
had just climbed back to the ground
when Rabbit came bounding up.

"What's happening?" asked Rabbit.

"I'm looking for a new home,"
explained Mole.
"Somewhere BEAUTIFUL."

"And SNUG," added Hedgehog.

"And SAFE," added Squirrel.

"I know just the place!"
said Rabbit.

Rabbit led Mole,
Squirrel and Hedgehog
to a little stream.

"Over here!" she said,
hopping easily
from stone to stone.

"So what do you think?"
said Rabbit, as they scrambled
into a hollow beside
a sparkling waterfall.

Mole tried to feel at home
in the hollow. But he kept
getting splashed.

"Well," he said, "it is very
BEAUTIFUL –
but it's too wet for me.
I'd like somewhere
a little more dry."

It was getting late and Mole
still hadn't found his new home.

"I didn't think it would
be this difficult," sighed Mole.

"Don't worry. We'll find somewhere," said Rabbit.

"We just need to give
it some thought," said Squirrel.

So they all sat down and thought,
and thought, and thought, until...

"I know just the place,"
said Mole.

He led Squirrel, Hedgehog
and Rabbit back across the woodland
to a familiar-looking hole.

"But this is your OLD home!"
said Rabbit, Hedgehog and Squirrel.

"I know," said Mole happily.
"Isn't it WONDERFUL?
It's not BIG or BRIGHT or BEAUTIFUL.
But it feels
just right to me."

It was dark outside, and a storm
was sweeping across the woodland.
But everyone was very
comfortable down
in Mole's burrow.

"It's so SNUG,"
said Hedgehog.

"And SAFE,"
said Squirrel.

"And DRY,"
said Rabbit.

"Yes," said Mole
contentedly.
"There's no place
like home!"

Other books by Jonathan Emmett and Vanessa Cabban

ISBN 987-1-4063-7304-2

ISBN 978-1-4063-7311-0

ISBN 978-1-4063-7324-0

ISBN 978-1-4063-7354-7

ISBN 978-1-4063-7353-0

ISBN 978-1-4063-2959-9

ISBN 978-1-4063-6549-8

Available from all good booksellers
www.walker.co.uk